# A SECRET IN THE FAMILY

*AN ADVENTIST GIRL STORY*

~ BOOK THREE ~

## JEAN BOONSTRA

**Pacific Press® Publishing Association**
Nampa, Idaho
Oshawa, Ontario, Canada
www.pacificpress.com

Edited by Tim Lale
Designed by Dennis Ferree
Cover illustration by Matthew Archambault

Additional copies of this book may be purchased at
http://www.adventistbookcenter.com

*Library of Congress Cataloging-in-Publication Data*

Boonstra, Jean Elizabeth.
    A secret in the family : Sarah 1842-1844 / Jean
Elizabeth Boonstra.
    p. cm. — (Adventist girl series; bk. 3)
    Summary: In 1843, ten-year-old Sarah Barnes
must deal with the excitement of a new baby,
competition with a classmate, a friend's tempo-
rary desertion, and confusion about her family's
belief in the imminent second comming of Jesus.
    ISBN: 0-8163-1887-5
    [1. Seventh-day Adventists 2. Family life 3. Second
Advent] I. Title.

    PZ7.B64613 Se 2002
    —dc21                          2001055170


05 06 • 5 4 3 2

# Contents

# Dedication

To my husband, Shawn, for his
constant love and encouragement.
To our daughter, Natalie, whose
birth on October 22, 1999
was a most joyous event.

CHAPTER 1

# The Barnes's Secret

On a cold Sunday afternoon in February of 1844, Sarah Barnes, now nine years old, and her friend Alannah Murphy lay on their backs on the hard wooden floor of Sarah's bedroom. Sarah closed her eyes and wiggled her toes in her slippers.

The Barnes's house felt cozy and warm. A fire was crackling in the hearth in the parlor. The sweet, cinnamon smell of apple pie floated up the stairs. Soon dinner would be ready. Outside, big wet snowflakes fell against the window. Slowly they melted and ran down the window in streams.

Sarah listened to her mother and father talking quietly in the parlor. Sunday afternoon was her favorite time of the week. Her father didn't work, and everyone was happy just to be together. Sarah yawned and closed her eyes. It was a wonderfully lazy afternoon.

Alannah looked toward the window, her hands behind her head. Her red curly hair spilled out all around her. Her soft voice floated through the air. "I love coming over to your house," she said.

"What did you say?" Sarah asked, yawning.

Alannah giggled. "Did you fall asleep? I said that I like coming over to your house on Sundays."

"I like it when you come over," said Sarah, sitting up and leaning against her bed. She rubbed her eyes. Maybe she had fallen asleep. She didn't remember exactly. "I like having company on Sundays. It is boring to just sit and talk to my sister all day."

"I get bored at home by myself with Mamó and Daideó," Alannah said. She rolled onto her stomach and put her chin in her hands. "Grandparents are great, but I miss my father."

Sarah felt thankful for her own family. She even felt guilty for kicking Katie out of their room when Alannah came over. She squeezed her friend's hand. "I'm sorry about your father," she said.

Alannah looked down at the floor.

"You must miss him a lot," Sarah said thoughtfully. She thought about her grandfather who had died the summer before. She still missed him. She couldn't imagine not having her mother or father.

Alannah sniffled. "I do."

They heard *knock, knock* at the door.

Sarah squeezed Alannah's hand again and then let go. "Come in," she said.

"Mother sent me up," Katie said, peeking around the door. Missy the cat scampered in around her feet. She pranced onto Katie's bed and curled up in a ball, licking her paws. "Dinner will be ready in fifteen minutes." Katie looked around the room. She hung on the door, swinging it back and forth. Then she added, "It's your turn to set the table."

"I know," Sarah said, "you don't have to remind me."

Alannah stood up. She picked up Sarah's violin from her chair and set it on the floor against the wall. "Do you want to keep me company while Sarah works?" she asked Katie as she sat down in the chair.

Katie looked at Alannah, then at Sarah. She didn't say anything. She just stared at her older sister with her big blue eyes.

Sarah giggled. "Well," she finally said, "come in. This is your room too."

Katie bounced through the door, swinging it closed behind her. She sat down on the floor and looked at Alannah. She hugged her legs to her chest.

Sarah smiled and pushed herself up off the floor. She walked over to the mirror and picked up her hairbrush. Smoothing her wispy brown hair, she pulled it back into a ponytail.

"Alannah, will you braid my hair for me?" Katie asked.

"I'd love to," Alannah replied, smiling. "Scoot over here and let me see what I can do."

Katie wiggled up against the chair. She pulled the ribbons from her straw-blond ponytails. "I'm ready," she said excitedly.

Sarah took off her shawl and tossed it onto her bed. "Have fun," she called over her shoulder. *It is nice to have a sister sometimes,* she thought, and tiptoed down the stairs.

The rest of the house was quiet. Mr. Barnes was sitting in his chair reading his Bible. Sarah stopped for a moment and watched him. His forehead was crinkled as he concentrated. Mrs. Barnes was stretched out on the sofa. Her long emerald-green dress was draped across the upholstery and touched the floor. Her feet rested on a pillow, and her eyes were closed.

Sarah slipped into the kitchen. She didn't need to ask Mother what needed to be done. She already knew.

The soup was bubbling and spitting in the heavy black pot hanging over the fire. Sarah lifted the wooden spoon off the mantle and stirred the soup. She peeked into the side oven. The pie was almost burnt! Quickly she pulled it out and set it on the kitchen table. *That was close,* she thought.

Sarah quietly and carefully opened the cupboard and pulled out the dishes. She lifted out the linen cloth and napkins her mother kept especially for Sunday dinner. She opened the tablecloth and lovingly spread it over the dining table. The crisp linen felt smooth under her fingers.

Mr. Barnes looked up from his reading. "Sarah," he said quietly, stretching his neck, "is it dinnertime already?" He marked his place and closed his Bible.

Sarah began setting out the soup bowls. "Almost," she whispered.

Mr. Barnes placed his Bible on the table beside his chair. He stood up, stretched, and leaned over Mrs. Barnes. "Margaret," he whispered.

Mrs. Barnes opened her eyes and sat up quickly. She almost knocked Mr. Barnes over. "I must've dozed off," she said, blinking her eyes and looking around the room. Suddenly she leaped up off the sofa. "The pie!"

Sarah laughed. "It's all right, Mother. I took it out. It smells delicious." She reached for the stack of napkins.

"Thank you," Mrs. Barnes said. She straightened her hair and walked into the kitchen. Slowly she lifted her apron off the hook on the wall. "I've been so tired the last few days," she said, yawning, and slipped the apron over her head. "I seem to be forgetting a lot of things."

"That's understandable," Mr. Barnes said as he stirred the fire with the poker, "considering your condition."

Sarah's arm froze, holding a linen napkin in mid-air. *I must've heard Father wrong,* she thought. Slowly she set the napkin down next to the soup bowl.

"Father," she asked carefully, "what did you just say?"

Mr. Barnes set the poker back on the hearth. Absentmindedly he answered, "I just said that considering your mother's condition—" He stopped and slowly turned around. Sheepishly he looked at Sarah and then at Mrs. Barnes. "Oops."

A rush of excitement sprang up inside Sarah. She ran to her mother and grabbed her hands.

# The Barnes's Secret

"Mother," she asked excitedly, "is it true? Are you having a baby?"

Mrs. Barnes sighed and looked over at Mr. Barnes. Then she put her arm around Sarah and pulled her close.

"We can't keep anything from you, can we, my curious one. Yes, we're having another baby."

Sarah couldn't believe it. She was very excited. Another baby! She hoped that it would be a boy—a baby brother.

Mr. Barnes put his hand on Sarah's shoulder. "Sorry," he whispered in his wife's ear.

Mrs. Barnes just shook her head. She took Sarah by the hand and guided her toward a chair. "Let's sit down," she said. "Edward, you too."

"Is everything all right, Mother?" Sarah asked.

"Yes," said Mrs. Barnes. Her soft hazel eyes seemed to smile at Sarah, reassuring her that it was true. "We don't want anyone to know about the new baby for a little while," she said, frowning a little at Mr. Barnes.

"No one else knows?" Sarah asked.

"No," said Mr. Barnes. "It needs to be our secret for a while."

Mrs. Barnes stroked Sarah's cheek. "We are counting on you," she said. "You are almost ten, and we know that you can keep our secret."

Sarah felt very grown up. She knew that she could keep their secret. "Does Grammy know?" she asked.

"No, not even Grammy knows," Mrs. Barnes said.

Mr. Barnes took Sarah's hand. He looked very serious. "You know, Sarah, that we believe Jesus is coming back very soon. He is going to take us to heaven with Him."

"Yes," Sarah answered. "We've been waiting for Jesus to come back for a while."

Mr. Barnes smiled. "There is still time,

my child. Our new baby may be born in heaven."

Mrs. Barnes's eyes sparkled. "A childbirth without pain," she said, "imagine that!"

The little kitchen door pushed open. "Hello," Grammy called from the kitchen.

"Can you keep our secret?" Mr. Barnes whispered.

"I promise," Sarah whispered back. She crossed her heart.

Mr. Barnes winked.

"It is freezing out there," said Grammy, shaking the snow off her shawl. "Is dinner ready?"

"Almost," said Mrs. Barnes, getting up from the table.

"Sarah, please call your sisters and Alannah for dinner. I'll finish setting the table."

Sarah skipped out of the kitchen. She was bursting with the good news. She wanted to tell the whole world, but she knew that she couldn't. Being part of her parents' secret made her feel special. A new baby! How wonderful!

Still absorbed in her thoughts, Sarah opened the bedroom door. Now Katie was brushing Alannah's hair. Alannah didn't seem to mind.

"Sarah, dolly!" Little Emily ran to her big sister. Her blond curls bounced. She was dragging Sarah's doll, Henrietta, on the floor behind her.

"Look who is up from her nap," Sarah said, scooping Emily up into her arms.

"Dolly!" said Emily enthusiastically, thrusting Henrietta into Sarah's face.

"Yes," said Sarah, taking her treasured doll out of her little sister's hands. "This is Sarah's doll. Now put her back on my bed, please," she said, setting Emily back down on the floor. "You have to ask before you play with her."

Emily batted her big blue eyes up at Sarah, but Sarah didn't budge. Emily gently put Henrietta back on Sarah's bed. "Sorry," she whispered.

"It's all right," Sarah said, picking Emily up again. "Dinner is ready," she said to Alannah and Katie.

"Do you like my hair?" Katie asked, twirling past her sister.

"It looks nice," said Sarah, smiling at Alannah.

Alannah shrugged her shoulders. "I did my best," she said.

"Let's go eat," said Sarah. Katie and Alannah bounced down ahead of her.

Sarah hugged Emily close. "I have a secret," she whispered into Emily's ear, "and I can't even tell you!"

Emily just giggled.

CHAPTER 2

# The
# Explosion

"I-m-a-g-i-n-a-r-y. Imaginary," Sarah said. She stood proudly at the front of her classroom.

"That is correct," Miss Button said. Sarah smiled and sat back down in her seat.

It was Friday afternoon, and as usual Sarah and her schoolmates were competing in a spelling bee. Sarah had been working hard all year on her spelling lessons. Her hard work was beginning to pay off. That day she and Nickie Cooper were the last two remaining in the game.

Miss Button read from the sheet in her hand. "Miss Cooper," she said, "your word is 'February.' "

Nickie walked to the front of the classroom and turned to face the class. She thrust out her chin and tossed her perfect curls over her shoulder.

"F-e-b-u-a-r-y. Febuary." She looked triumphantly around the room.

Miss Button stood up from her desk.

"I'm afraid that your answer is incorrect. 'February' is spelled F-e-b-r-u-a-r-y. You missed the 'r.' You may be seated, Miss Cooper."

Sarah couldn't believe her good luck. Nickie's face turned bright red. She rushed to her seat and stared down at her desk.

"For the first time in several months we have a new winner," Miss Button said, her kind eyes smiling. "Congratulations, Miss Barnes. Good work."

Sarah was delighted. Finally she had

# The Explosion

beaten Nickie. *Wait until I tell Mother and Father,* she thought. *They'll be so proud!*

"Thank you, Miss Button," she answered politely.

Miss Button smiled. "You may all be dismissed now," she said to the class. "See you on Monday. Good afternoon."

"Good afternoon, Miss Button," the class answered.

A bustle of activity filled the room as everyone scrambled for their books and empty lunch pails. Sarah's best friend, Pam Van Dyke, twirled around in her seat. "You did it," she said, her eyes shimmering with excitement.

Nickie stood up from the desk she shared with Pam. Her icy blue eyes met Sarah's. Sarah shivered. "Congratulations," said Nickie. "You won't win next time."

Sarah was still too excited from her win to let her feelings be hurt. "I just might win again," she stammered as Nickie brushed past her.

"Don't worry about her," Pam said. She slipped her arm through Sarah's. "She is just jealous!"

Alannah grabbed Sarah's other arm. "I still can't believe that you did it," she sang happily.

Sarah smiled as she and Pam and Alannah walked home from school. She didn't even notice the frost nipping at her nose. She was too happy. They stopped at Alannah's house for a cup of cocoa, and then Sarah and Pam dashed back out into the cold, gray afternoon.

"Goodbye, Pam," Sarah called as Pam swung open the gate and walked up the path leading to her house. Pam waved over her shoulder.

Sarah almost skipped the rest of the way home. It felt so good to have beaten Nickie. Sarah dashed up the front path and into the warmth of her home.

"What about President Tyler?" Mrs. Barnes called from the kitchen.

# The Explosion

"He was fine," Mr. Barnes called back from the parlor. He sat in his chair next to the fire, reading *The New Hampshire Gazette*. Sarah loved coming home from school in the winter. Most days her father was already inside. In the summer he often worked outside until well after she was in bed.

"I'm home," Sarah called, hanging her coat and scarf on the peg next to the door.

"Well," said Mrs. Barnes, coming out of the kitchen and drying a big wooden bowl with a tea towel. Emily toddled out behind her. She carried her own tea towel and a little wooden bowl. "Our spelling champion is here!" Mrs. Barnes's face lit up with pride.

Sarah's heart sank. "How do you know?" she asked. "I wanted to surprise you after supper."

Mrs. Barnes hugged her tight. "You can blame your little sister," she said, kissing the top of her head. "She was so excited she just about burst when she came home from school."

"Congratulations," Mr. Barnes said. He hugged Sarah with one arm, his newspaper tucked under the other.

Sarah was happy that her parents were pleased. "It's not a big thing," she said.

The kitchen door crashed open. "I'm done milking Pepper," hollered Katie. The sound of the milk pail slamming onto the table rang out in the kitchen. A loud *splash* and a "Whoops" from Katie followed it.

Sarah rolled her eyes.

"Some things never change," Mrs. Barnes said with a wink.

Mr. Barnes laughed and carried his newspaper back into the parlor. "Girls," he said, looking over his shoulder, "come here for a minute, please. Something important has happened, and I want to tell you about it."

Katie skipped out of the kitchen. "Good spelling," she said when she saw Sarah.

# The Explosion

"Thanks for blabbing," Sarah said.

Katie looked hurt. Instantly Sarah felt bad for being mean. Katie was just excited, after all. "Did you see Nickie's red face?" she asked nicely.

Katie smiled and then giggled. "I sure did." She followed Sarah into the parlor.

Mr. Barnes opened the newspaper again. "A few days ago, on the twenty-eighth of February, there was a big explosion on a Navy ship," he told them. His eyebrows crinkled together. "The Secretary of State was killed, and so were many other important government workers."

"Father," Sarah said, not really wanting to interrupt him.

"Yes," said Mr. Barnes, lowering the newspaper to look at her.

"Miss Button told us about the explosion this morning. President Tyler is safe, isn't he?"

Mr. Barnes looked pleased. "Why, yes," he said. "President Tyler was on the ship, but he didn't get hurt. We need to remember the families of those who were killed. This is a terrible tragedy."

"Yes, Father," said Sarah and Katie at once.

Mr. Barnes folded the newspaper in half. "Miss Button is a good teacher to keep you up to date on what is happening in the world."

Sarah smiled. "I know she is," she said.

Mr. Barnes chuckled. "Now, Sarah, go upstairs and practice your violin. Katie, help your mother."

"Thank you, Father," they answered politely.

Sarah strolled into her room. She felt happy and carefree. She picked up her violin and tucked it under her chin. *This is going to be a good weekend,* she thought, smiling.

* * * * *

On Sunday morning Sarah sat in her usual place in the little Methodist church

# The Explosion

in Portsmouth. She squirmed in the pew. She tried to concentrate on the sermon, but it was no use. Her mind kept wandering.

It had been several months since Pastor Robinson left. Sarah missed him very much. For a while the church had no pastor. Several of the elders of the church took turns preaching. It had been fun. Then the new pastor arrived, and everyone was delighted. Everyone, that is, except Sarah.

"Jesus said, 'Rise, take up thy bed, and walk'!" Pastor MacMillan lifted his Bible high into the air. His tall frame loomed behind the pulpit.

Sarah pushed herself up in her seat. The story of the lame man was one of her favorite Bible stories. Still, she couldn't concentrate. There was just something about Pastor MacMillan that she didn't like. Sarah crinkled up her nose, crossed her arms, and watched him as he spoke. Pastor MacMillan's dark-gray beard and bushy side burns nearly covered his face. Sarah couldn't see his eyes. He certainly didn't smile.

Sarah sighed. *I miss Pastor Robinson,* she thought.

"Mother," Sarah whispered, tapping her mother on the arm. "May I be excused?"

Mrs. Barnes looked worried. "Why, are you ill?" she asked, putting the back of her hand on Sarah's forehead.

"No," Sarah answered, swinging her legs back and forth.

Mrs. Barnes quickly put her hand on Sarah's leg. "You sit still, and you may not leave church unless you are ill, or it is an emergency," she whispered sharply. "Have I made myself clear?"

"Yes, Mother," Sarah said. She slumped in her seat. *It's no use,* she thought. *I'm stuck here forever!* She stared at the stained-glass window at the back of the church. Slowly she counted the red pieces of glass. "One, two, three …"

# The Explosion

"Our closing hymn this morning is number 329. Please stand," said Pastor MacMillan.

*Finally,* thought Sarah.

The little church swelled with music and singing. Sarah felt a little better. Pastor MacMillan said the closing prayer.

"You may be seated," said Pastor MacMillan. He placed his Bible on the pulpit and nodded toward the back of the church. "Mrs. Cooper has an announcement."

Mrs. Cooper swished up the aisle. Her satin dress trailed on the floor, and her ribbon-covered hat was perched elegantly on her head. She stood behind the pulpit and looked proudly across the church. "Please stay for tea," she said importantly. "We would like to officially welcome our pastor to Portsmouth."

As Mrs. Cooper swished back down the aisle, the organ played.

Sarah picked up her shawl and was

about to stand up, when her mother put her hand on her knee.

"Don't go anywhere," Mrs. Barnes whispered. "I want to talk to you."

Sarah's heart sank. Mother wanting to talk was usually not good news.

"Mother," Mrs. Barnes whispered to Grammy, "will you take Katie and Emily to the tea, please? I need to talk to Sarah."

Grammy put on her gloves. "I suppose that I could," she said, hesitating.

"Thank you," said Mrs. Barnes, pushing Emily toward her. She didn't want to give Grammy a chance to change her mind.

Emily bounced up and down. "Grammy, Grammy!" she said at the top of her voice.

"Now settle down, child," said Grammy, looking around embarrassed. "Do be careful of my dress. You are stepping all over it."

Emily pouted and put her hands behind her back. Grammy took her hand and led her out.

# The Explosion

"Have fun," Katie whispered sarcastically, following behind them.

Sarah scowled.

A woman whom Sarah only vaguely recognized stopped at their pew. Nervously she said, "Mr. Barnes. I'm terribly sorry to trouble you, but may I have a word with you." She wrung her hands together.

"Of course," Mr. Barnes said. "Excuse me, Margaret."

Mrs. Barnes nodded, and Mr. Barnes gently led the young woman to the front pew.

Sarah was used to this. Father was an elder in the church. Often he stayed after the service to talk to someone. He liked helping people.

Mr. and Mrs. Van Dyke, and then Pam and her brother Peter walked down the aisle.

"Good day, Mrs. Barnes," Pam said.

"Good day, Pamela," Mrs. Barnes replied, smiling pleasantly. "I'm afraid that Sarah won't be able to come to the tea just yet. She'll see you in a little while."

"Yes'm," Pam said. " 'Bye, then."

*This is just great,* thought Sarah. *Now Pam knows that I'm in trouble.*

Mrs. Barnes waited until the church was almost empty. Then she turned and looked at Sarah. "You know why we're here, don't you?" she asked.

Sarah nodded. She sat on her hands and looked down at her feet.

"Why have you been so disruptive in church the last few weeks?" Mrs. Barnes asked. "It isn't like you. You usually love church."

"Not anymore," Sarah said.

Mrs. Barnes looked hurt. "Why?" she asked.

"I don't like Pastor MacMillan," Sarah finally blurted out. She hadn't meant to say it. It just came out.

"Sarah! I'm disappointed in you," Mrs. Barnes said. "You are much more grown up than that."

# The Explosion

Sarah looked deep into her mother's hazel eyes. "He isn't friendly, and he preaches stuff that isn't true." Sarah mustered up all her courage. "Last week he said that there are going to be a thousand years of peace, and then Jesus will come again."

Mrs. Barnes sighed. "I know, love," she said, taking Sarah's hand. "Not everyone in this church believes that Jesus is coming again soon, including Pastor MacMillan. But he is our pastor, and we must love and respect him. He is one of God's workers."

"Jesus is coming again soon, isn't He, Mother?" Sarah asked. A teardrop gathered in the corner of her eye. Quickly she blinked it away.

Mrs. Barnes instinctively put her hand on her stomach. "Yes," she answered. "The Second Advent will likely be here within a month." Mrs. Barnes stared dreamily across the church.

"I haven't told anyone," said Sarah quietly.

Mrs. Barnes looked confused for a moment. Then she quickly pulled her hand off her swelling abdomen. She gave Sarah a hug. "I know you haven't," she said. "I trust you."

The woman that had asked to speak to Mr. Barnes walked briskly down the aisle. A smile danced across her face. Mr. Barnes sat down in the pew in front of Sarah and Mrs. Barnes.

"That was uplifting," he said, his face all aglow. "Miss Ramsey now believes in the soon coming of our Lord."

"Edward," said Mrs. Barnes happily, clapping her hands together.

Mr. Barnes's eyes welled up with tears. "It seems that the explosion on the Navy ship this week made her think. It reminded her of the power Satan still has on this world. She felt she needed to study more, and now accepts that Jesus is coming within the month."

"How wonderful," Mrs. Barnes said. "Thank You, Lord."

# The Explosion

Sarah watched shyly as her father wiped away his tears. The only time she ever saw tears in his eyes was at moments like this.

Sarah felt happy again. Still, though, something was bothering her. *Within a month,* she thought. Suddenly, the nearness of the Second Coming was very real to her. The words rang in her head. *Within a month. Within a month.*

## CHAPTER 3

# The Thunderstorm

Sarah eagerly burst into the afternoon sunshine. "It's my turn to skip," she called, running down the schoolhouse steps and out onto the green grassy field. She handed Pam and Alannah each one end of the jump rope.

"All right," Pam said, laughing, "but we're going to make you work hard!"

Sarah laughed and jumped under the swinging rope. It felt good after having been inside all afternoon. Sarah's petticoats bounced with each jump. The warm spring breeze tickled her bare legs.

The month that Mr. Barnes had said that Jesus would return within had already passed. It was now the first week of April. The apple blossoms were already bursting forth on the apple trees, and the finches sang in the meadow beside the rushing waters of the river. Mr. Barnes had said that Jesus was going to return very soon. He said that it would be the next great event to take place. Sarah waited each day. But each day was full of the same ordinary things.

"George Washington never told a lie," Pam and Alannah sang out loudly, "'till he ran around the corner…"

Sarah hopped out from under the rope, ran around Alannah, and jumped back in.

"And stole a cherry pie," they sang. "How many cherries were in that pie? 1, 2, 3, 4 …"

Nickie waltzed across the grassy field and stared at Sarah as she jumped. "You're going to miss," she called, cupping her hands to her mouth.

"15, 16, 17…" Pam and Alannah continued.

Sarah tried to ignore Nickie, but she couldn't help herself. "I am not," she bragged, turning her head. Just as she turned, she stumbled. "Humbug!" she muttered.

Nickie and then Pam and Alannah laughed. Pam gathered up the jump rope and handed it to Sarah. Embarrassed, Sarah shoved it into her pocket.

"Alannah," Nickie said, smiling, "I love your new hair ribbon." She admired Alannah's soft green ribbon. "It looks lovely against your hair."

"Thank you," said Alannah, touching it with her fingers.

Nickie straightened her back and looked around as if the whole school ground could hear her. "Why are you still friends with these two losers?" she said loudly to Alannah. "They think that they are going to go fly away to heaven any minute. They think that they're better than us."

Alannah didn't say anything.

Sarah and Pam just looked at each other. *Maybe if no one says anything she'll go away,* Sarah thought.

Nickie didn't give up. "Alannah," she said even more loudly, "Sarah and Pam are just followers of that mad man, Mr. Miller. My father says that the old man is crazy and should be committed to a lunatic hospital. He said that Jesus was supposed to come back more than a month ago. Where is He?" Nickie stretched out her arms and looked up into the sky.

Alannah started to say something, but before she could speak, Sarah twirled around.

"Mr. Miller is not a mad man," she said, looking Nickie straight in the eye. "He is a kind old man who loves Jesus. I believe that he is right."

"So do I," said Pam, stepping up beside Sarah.

# The Thunderstorm

Alannah looked down at her shoes. Sarah waited, but Alannah didn't say anything. Alannah looked up awkwardly. She looked past Sarah and toward the school steps. "Look!" she cried. "Miss Button brought Redmond over!"

Nickie and Alannah seemed to instantly forget about the argument. Sarah smoldered inside. *Why didn't Alannah defend us?* she wondered. She followed them over to the school steps. She did want to see Redmond.

Sarah gently nudged her way to the front of the crowd that gathered around Miss Button. "Oh, Reddy," she said, scratching the Irish setter between the ears. "You are getting so big."

The little dog wagged his tail and panted happily.

Miss Button's friendly young face smiled. "He is getting big," she said. Her eyes twinkled. "He is going to eat me out of house and home!"

Sarah laughed.

Everyone clambered on top of one another to get their chance to see the dog. "All right," said Miss Button at last, "I think that everyone has seen Reddy. You should be going home now, or your parents will wonder what happened to you!"

"Miss Button," Sarah asked quietly as everyone got up to leave, "Do you believe that Jesus is still coming soon?"

Miss Button smiled and patted Reddy on the head. "Yes, I do," she said softly. She winked. "Now you better get going home, Miss Barnes. Your friends are waiting for you."

Sarah skipped over to Alannah and Pam. Her feet seemed lighter underneath her than they had a few minutes ago.

"Isn't Reddy still so cute?" said Alannah.

"He is the cutest dog ever," Sarah said.

Sarah, Alannah, and Pam walked home together. They talked about all sorts of things. But they didn't talk about the fight with Nickie.

Sarah dashed down the road toward home. She was late, and she didn't want to get into trouble. She ran around the side of the house. *I'll just slip into the kitchen*, she thought, *and no one will know that I'm late.*

"Sarah, Sarah!" Emily ran to welcome her big sister. She carried a wooden spoon in her hand and had dirt all over her face.

"You've been helping Mother in the garden, I see," said Sarah, kissing Emily on the only clean spot left on her face. *Of all the days for Mother to be working in the garden,* she thought, her heart sinking.

"Emily gardening," said Emily proudly.

Mrs. Barnes stood up and stretched her back. "You're late," she said to Sarah. "Grammy started peeling the potatoes. Go inside quickly and help her." Mrs. Barnes picked up the shovel. "You know how much she hates cooking!"

Sarah set Emily down and dashed

around the neatly weeded rows of carrots and radishes. "Yes, Mother. Sorry."

The next few hours were a blur of cooking, dishes, and homework. Somehow, Sarah managed to get everything done. At long last she sat down on the sofa in the parlor next to her mother. She didn't have the energy to do another thing. She glanced down at her stitching sampler and turned up her nose.

"Are you going to read here, or maybe work on your stitching, Sarah?" Mrs. Barnes asked as she stitched up a hole in her husband's work pants.

"I don't think so," Sarah said, yawning. "I think that I'll go to bed and read. I'm tired."

"You and your father both," said Mrs. Barnes giggling. She nodded toward Mr. Barnes's chair. He was slumped over, sound asleep.

"He looks uncomfortable," Sarah said.

"He chopped all the ice off the pond and packed it down into the cold room today,"

# The Thunderstorm

answered Mrs. Barnes, reaching for her shears. "It's hard work."

Sarah nodded. "Good night, Mother," she said, covering her mouth as another yawn escaped.

"Good night."

Sarah dragged herself upstairs. She poured some water into the wash basin. She washed her face and hands and put on her nightgown. It was nice to go to bed before Katie. She didn't have to fight for the mirror.

Sarah kneeled down beside her bed and said her prayers. She crawled underneath the blankets and let her head fall onto her pillow. She closed her eyes, and before she had a chance to think about it she was sound asleep.

*Crash! Boom!*

Sarah sat straight up in bed.

*Crash!* The house shook, and a flash of lightning lit up the room.

Sarah was still more asleep than she was awake. The room became dark and quiet again. Then, without warning, lightning flashed in the room again.

Sarah watched Katie hop out of bed, with Missy in her arms, and dash out of the door. Sarah instinctively grabbed Henrietta and ran after Katie in the dark. *It's really here,* she thought. She was terrified. *The end of the world is really here! This isn't how I expected it to be at all!* Another clap of thunder shook the house as she scurried down the hall.

Without even thinking about what she was doing, Sarah ran into her mother and father's room. She jumped right into the middle of the bed and landed with a big thud on top of someone's leg.

"Ow!" yelled Mr. Barnes. He sat up and looked around him, dazed.

"Sarah!" said Mrs. Barnes. "Good heavens! What on earth is the matter?" She sat up on her side of the bed. Katie was snuggled beside her. Missy was still in her arms.

"Mother, Father," said Sarah. "The end of the world is here! It really is!"

# The Thunderstorm

Mr. Barnes pushed himself up to a sitting position. He rubbed his eyes. "Come here," he said.

Sarah snuggled in between her mother and father. "It's just a thunderstorm, sweetheart," said Mr. Barnes gently.

Sarah blinked her eyes. She looked at the window and saw the rain splashing against it. Another thunderclap, this one a little quieter, sounded. Sarah took a deep breath. *I feel stupid now,* she thought.

"I knew that it was a thunderstorm," Katie said, poking her head out around her mother.

"I see that we have the whole family in here," Mr. Barnes said. "We even have the cat in bed with us!"

Mrs. Barnes sighed. "Not quite the whole family," she said.

Just as she said it, Emily began to cry. "Mama!" she called.

Mr. Barnes raised his hands up in the air and let them drop to his side. Everyone stared at each other for a minute, and then they started to giggle.

"I'll go and get her," said Mr. Barnes. "I'm awake anyway."

He carried little Emily into the bed. She giggled and bounced, as refreshed as if it were morning.

"Now we really do have the *whole* family here, don't we, Mother?" Sarah said.

"Yes, we really do," said Mrs. Barnes, holding out her hand protectively as Emily crashed toward her. Mrs. Barnes grabbed Emily and hugged her. "Sarah," she said, looking at her husband, "why don't you tell your sisters our good news."

Emily jumped up and down. The cat flew onto the floor. "Good news! Good news!" she sang.

"Do you mean it?" Sarah asked.

"Sure," said Mr. Barnes, winking at his wife.

"Well," Sarah said, pausing dramatically. "We're having another baby!"

# The Thunderstorm

"Oh!" Katie said. "Why didn't anyone tell me?"

Mr. Barnes laughed. "It's a long story," he answered.

Katie frowned and then smiled. "I guess that it's all right," she said. "When will the baby be born?"

Mrs. Barnes smiled. "If time continues, then in early August."

A flash of lightning shone for a moment in the room. Sarah remembered her fear of just a few minutes before. The look on her face must have reminded Mr. Barnes, too. He put his arm around Sarah and Mrs. Barnes and Katie. He pulled Emily onto his lap. "The end of the world won't be scary like a thunderstorm," he reassured them. "It will be brilliant and beautiful. It may seem scary to those who aren't ready for it, but we are ready. We should look eagerly for Jesus' coming."

"Yes, Father," Sarah answered bravely. But when she looked out of the window at the blowing rain, she didn't feel so sure.

## CHAPTER 4

# The Last Day of School

"David Cooper. Peter Van Dyke," Mrs. Button called out.

Proudly David and Peter walked to the front of the classroom. It was the last day of school for the year. The warm summer air rushed through the open windows and filled the classroom. Miss Button handed David a certificate.

"Congratulations," she said, shaking David's hand.

David smiled awkwardly and pushed

up his glasses. "Thank you," he said and bowed.

Miss Button handed Peter his certificate and shook his hand. "Congratulations, Mr. Van Dyke," she said, smiling.

Peter's face shone. He grinned, and his rosy cheeks glowed in the afternoon sunlight. "Thank you, Miss Button," he said, bowing enthusiastically.

"Students," said Miss Button, her long apron sweeping the floor as she turned. "Next year will be David and Peter's last year in school. They will be our oldest students next year." Miss Button motioned for the two boys to sit down. "Congratulations, young men."

Sarah swung her legs back and forth under the bench. The last day of school was an important day, and she was wearing her Sunday dress. She pulled at her sleeves. The arms felt tight. Sarah was too excited to sit still. Miss Button called the next group of students to the front. She handed them each a certificate and shook their hand. "We're next," she whispered to Alannah.

"Sit still," said Alannah, a little annoyed. She looked at Sarah's swinging legs and sneered. She turned and stared straight ahead.

Sarah felt hurt. *I wonder what's the matter with Alannah?* she thought. She wasn't nearly as excited as she had been a moment ago.

"Miss Barnes, Miss Cooper, Miss Murphy, and Miss Van Dyke," Miss Button called.

Sarah walked to the front of the classroom. She tried to be excited again, but she had a sick feeling in the bottom of her stomach.

"Congratulations," said Miss Button, handing Sarah her certificate and shaking her hand.

"Thank you," said Sarah. She smiled and curtsied.

Miss Button handed Nickie her certificate. Nickie's yellow curls glimmered against her new dress. It was beautiful. It was white with blue ribbons and tiny blue bows stitched all over it. Sarah was jealous. She had never had such a beautiful dress.

"Thank you, Miss Button," Nickie said, curtsying. Her dress swept along the wooden floor.

Alannah and Pam both received their certificates and curtsied.

As Sarah sat down in her desk, her eyes met Alannah's. Quickly, Alannah looked away.

"Did you notice Nickie's dress?" Sarah whispered to her nervously. "I wish that I had her clothes."

"I suppose," Alannah said.

Sarah's heart sank. *What did I do?* she thought. *Why is Alannah mad at me?* Hot burning tears gathered in her eyes. Sarah blinked hard. She wasn't excited anymore.

# The Last Day of School

All she could think about was Alannah.

Miss Button stood at the front of the classroom. She put her hands together. Her pleasant face glowed with pride. "Thank you, students, for a wonderful school year. I look forward to seeing you back next year. May God bless you all."

"God bless you, Miss Button," the class answered.

"You may be dismissed," Miss Button said. She smiled and sat down behind her desk.

Pam jumped up. Her blond curls bounced up and down. She put her arm through Sarah's and dragged her toward the door. "Let's go," she said. "Let's play George Washington. I was up to 55 cherries this morning."

Sarah tried to protest, but Pam dragged her out onto the schoolyard. Pam dug the jumping rope out of her pocket.

Nickie and Alannah glided down the steps. Alannah's red hair sparkled.

Pam threw one end of the well-used rope to Sarah.

"Alannah," she called. "Come on. Let's play George Washington."

"Not today," said Alannah. "I'm going over to Nicole's house."

Pam looked shocked. She looked at Sarah. Sarah shrugged her shoulders.

"Since when is she 'Nicole'?" Pam asked, her cheeks flushed.

"Since always," interrupted Nickie. She stepped over the jump rope and past Pam. Alannah followed behind her. "If you knew anything about me, you would know that I prefer 'Nicole'."

"Goodbye, *Nicole*," Pam said sarcastically. "Bye, Alannah," she called hesitatingly. Neither Nickie nor Alannah turned to say goodbye. They walked away, their hair blowing in the summer breeze.

"Alannah hates us, I guess," Pam said, sitting down on the grass.

# The Last Day of School

Sarah sat down next to her. "I know," she said. "I can't figure out what happened."

Katie ran toward them. "May I skip with you?" she asked, leaping up and down. "Please, Sarah!"

"We're not skipping," Pam said. She put the rope back into her pocket.

"Suit yourself," Katie said and ran toward the group of girls playing jacks under the maple tree.

"Let's go home," Sarah said. She hung her head.

They walked across the schoolyard toward home. Neither of them spoke. They didn't have to. They were both thinking about the same thing.

Meanwhile, Alannah and Nickie walked toward Nickie's house.

"I knew that you'd finally get rid of those two," said Nickie triumphantly. She took out two lollipops from her lunch pail and handed one to Alannah. "My mother and father say that the Barneses and the Van Dykes are a crazy lot nowadays. They are not to be trusted."

"They may believe that strange stuff about the end of the world," Alannah answered, "but I'm not sure that they aren't still my friends. I'm listening to you today, but don't think that I won't change my mind." Alannah popped the lollipop into her mouth. She furrowed her eyebrows and marched along beside Nickie.

\* \* \* \* \*

Sarah slipped into the house. She tried to sneak upstairs but couldn't.

"Sarah," Mrs. Barnes called from the kitchen. "Come here!"

Sarah dropped her copybook and her stitching sampler by the door. Her mother and Grammy were talking in the kitchen.

"Remember this one," Mrs. Barnes said, holding up a tiny nightgown. "It seems as though it were yesterday that Sarah was this small."

Grammy sipped her tea. "Yes," she said. "I remember how excited your father was to have a granddaughter. Sarah was always very special to him."

Sarah stepped into the kitchen. "Yes, Mother," she said, "you called."

"Sarah, love," said Mrs. Barnes cheerfully. Her round stomach pushed out the pleats in her apron. "We're going through the baby things." Mrs. Barnes carefully unfolded a little bonnet. "I thought that you might like to help."

"No, thank you," Sarah said. "I'm going to change my clothes."

"Fine then," said Mrs. Barnes without looking up. "Oh, look at this one," she said to Grammy. She held up a small hand-knit sweater. "You made this one for Katie."

Grammy touched the little sweater gently with her fingers. "I'd almost forgotten about it," she said.

# A SECRET IN THE FAMILY

Sarah climbed the stairs. *What a rotten day,* she thought. *Alannah hates me, and Mother doesn't even care about my last day of school.*

Sarah hung her good dress in the closet. She thought about Nickie's new dress. Frowning, she reached for her everyday dress and apron. She pulled them on and threw herself onto her bed. She didn't make a sound, but hot salty tears ran down her cheeks. Sarah hugged Henrietta close. She wiped the tears away with the back of her hand.

Knock, knock.

Sarah rolled over and faced the wall.

"Come in," she said quietly.

"Sarah," said Mrs. Barnes softly. "Are you all right?"

"Yes, Mother," she replied, not turning around.

Mrs. Barnes sat gently on the edge of the bed. She stroked Sarah's hair. "I didn't ask you how your last day of school was. How was it?" she asked.

# The Last Day of School

"Fine," Sarah said. She sniffled.

"Would you like to talk about it?" Mrs. Barnes asked, still gently stroking Sarah's hair.

Sarah wanted to. She wanted to tell her mother everything. She wanted to cry and climb up into her mother's lap the way she did when she was little. Instead she said, "No, thank you."

Mrs. Barnes patted her softly on her back. "All right," she said. "I'm here if you change your mind."

Sarah listened as her mother closed the door behind her. She sobbed into her pillow. Now she felt worse! She dried her tears and picked up her violin. She found one of her favorite pieces and began to play. She played and played, and tried to forget about her day.

"Sarah," hollered Katie, throwing the door open. "Mother says to tell you to go and help her in the kitchen when you're done practicing."

Sarah set her violin down. "Fine," she snapped. "You don't have to yell."

"Fine," said Katie. She pulled off her good dress and put on an old dress and apron. She dashed out of the door again as quickly as she had come in.

Sarah sighed and picked up Katie's dress off the floor. She draped it neatly across the bed. *I'm certainly not hanging it up for her,* she thought.

The sweet aroma of strawberries filled the kitchen. Mrs. Barnes was stirring a pot full of strawberry jam. Little hairs peaked out from under her cap and curled up and stuck to her skin. A neat pile of baby clothes sat next to the back door. Katie sat at the kitchen table measuring pieces of twine to make candles.

"Sarah," said Mrs. Barnes, spotting her out of the corner of her eye. "Please come and watch this jam. Keep stirring it so that it doesn't burn." Mrs. Barnes handed Sarah the long-handled wooden spoon. "I'll get the canning jars ready," she said. She wiped her forehead with the back of her hand.

Sarah took the spoon without complaining. She stirred the sweet syrupy jam.

"Excuse me," Katie said. She reached around past Sarah and pulled a pot of bubbling fat from beside the pot of jam. She had long mitts on both hands to protect her from the splatters.

"Be careful with that," Sarah said, stepping to the side. "It is very hot."

"I'm fine," said Katie confidently.

Sarah watched as Katie set the hot fat on the table and dipped a piece of twine into and through it. Making candles was a slow and messy job. *I'm glad that's not my job anymore,* Sarah thought, stirring the jam.

"What a busy household!" The kitchen door swung open, and Mr. Barnes stepped inside.

"Edward!" said Mrs. Barnes, drying a jar with a clean tea towel. "This is a surprise."

"I had to get out of the sun," Mr. Barnes said, taking off his hat and running his arm across his forehead. "Do you have any lemonade?"

Mrs. Barnes poured a tall glass of lemonade for her husband. Mr. Barnes drank it down in one long gulp and set the empty glass on the counter. "That hit the spot," he said. "I've almost got the corn crop in for the year," he said, kicking off his boots. "That sun is a scorcher. I'm going to lie down in the parlor for a bit."

"Yes, dear," said Mrs. Barnes absent-mindedly as she dried the last jar. "Sarah, how does that jam look?"

"Fine," said Sarah. She was still feeling cranky.

Mrs. Barnes set a thick wooden board on the counter. She carried the pot of jam over and set it down on the board. Sarah followed her. Mrs. Barnes handed her a ladle, and together they filled jars with the hot jam.

"Ouch!" Katie screamed at the top of her lungs.

Sarah was so frightened she jumped and almost knocked over the pot of bubbling jam.

"Mother, help!" Katie screamed.

Katie stood beside the kitchen table holding her arm. It was bright red. Mother grabbed a tea towel and dipped it into the cool drinking water. She placed it on Katie's arm.

"What happened?" Mr. Barnes asked, running in.

"Katie burned her arm in the hot fat for the candles," Mrs. Barnes said calmly. "Sarah, run and get me the ointment and a clean sheet." She kissed Katie's head. Katie buried her face in her mother's shoulder. "Now, love," said Mrs. Barnes soothingly. "Everything will be all right."

Frantically Sarah ran to her parents' bedroom. She threw open the closet and pulled the ointment and a sheet off the shelf. She flew back downstairs. Mrs. Barnes quickly rubbed the ointment on and tore a strip off the sheet and wrapped it around Katie's arm.

Katie sniffled. "Is that better now?" asked Mrs. Barnes.

"A little," Katie whimpered.

Sarah sat down. She felt shaky. Maybe it was Katie's accident, or perhaps it was the fight with Alannah, but her stomach was aching. Sarah felt angry. She tried to calm down, but it was no use. The anger took over. She felt confused and shaky and boiling mad all at once. She knew that she probably shouldn't say anything, but before she could stop them, the words tumbled out.

"What is going on?" she exclaimed to no one in particular. "Is Jesus coming back soon or isn't He?" Her cheeks flushed. "Father is putting in the crops," she said, looking at Mr. Barnes, who was leaning against the table. "Mother is making more jam than we'll ever eat in a thousand years. Katie still has to make candles even though it is the beginning of summer!" Katie looked up at her sister with wide eyes. "I think that Nickie Cooper is right," Sarah exploded. "We are all crazy. I don't like it!"

Sarah sat down in her chair in a crumpled heap. The boiling feeling was gone. Now she just felt confused.

Mr. Barnes put his hand strongly on her shoulder. "You look at me right now, young lady," he said. His voice was stern.

Sarah looked up at her father's angry face.

"First," he began, "I don't care if you are ten years old. You do not ever speak in that tone again. Is that clear?"

"Yes, Father," Sarah said. The tears rolled down her cheeks.

Mr. Barnes's face softened. He pulled up

69

a chair and took a deep breath as he sat down. "Now," he said gently. "Tell me what is the matter."

"Just what I said," Sarah replied. "I don't know if Jesus is coming again or not. I'm confused. I don't know what to expect. Everyone is acting like we're going to be here forever."

Mr. Barnes took her hand in his. "When we're done talking I want you to take my Bible and read Luke 19. That chapter tells us that until Jesus comes we are to keep at our work here on earth. We are to prepare as if we are going to be here for many years. But our hearts should always be looking eagerly for Jesus' coming."

Sarah sniffled. "Thank you, Father."

"Anything else you would like to share?" Mr. Barnes asked lovingly.

"Alannah hates me," Sarah blubbered. The tears started again and fell onto her lap. "Nickie finally convinced her that we're crazy. We're not, are we, Father?"

Mr. Barnes hugged her close. "No, we're not," he said. "We're not."

Mrs. Barnes put down the tea towel and rubbed Sarah's back. She pulled Sarah away from Mr. Barnes's hug and wiped her cheeks. "If there is one thing I know about good friends," she said, "it is that small disagreements can't keep them apart. Alannah is your good friend. It will all work out. Just give it a little time."

Sarah hugged her mother. "I hope so," she said between sobs. "I really, really hope so!"

## CHAPTER 5

# Summertime Fun

A few weeks later, on Sunday morning, Sarah and her family slipped into their usual pew in church. Sarah looked at the familiar faces all around her. Pam and Peter sat next to their parents in their usual spot. Sarah giggled as she watched Pam stick her elbow hard into Peter's arm. Peter was about to holler, but Pam put her finger to her lips and shushed him. She glanced over her shoulder to see if anyone had seen them. Her eyes met Sarah's. She waved. Her bright blue eyes danced in the morning brightness.

Sarah waved back at her best friend. *I'm glad that I can always count on Pam*, she thought. She giggled again. *Poor Peter's arm!*

The organ played, and the elders and Pastor MacMillan walked to the front of the church. Sarah watched Pastor MacMillan pick up a hymnal and hand it to the man beside him. Instead of singing, Pastor MacMillan studied the notes in his hand. He didn't seem to notice the congregation sitting in front of him.

Pastor MacMillan boomed out the morning's sermon. It was difficult to sit still, but Sarah managed. At long last the service was over. Sarah took Emily by the hand and followed Mr. Barnes out of their aisle.

"Good day, Mr. Barnes," said Pastor MacMillan, shaking his hand. He didn't smile. "I've been meaning to come and visit your family. Perhaps we could visit at the picnic this afternoon."

"Of course, pastor," Mr. Barnes answered in his friendliest voice. "That would be just fine."

Sarah pushed her way through the people and out of the foyer. Pam caught up to her. "Do you want to ride with us to the picnic?" she asked.

"I can't," Sarah replied, grabbing Emily by the arm before she could run away. "I promised my mother that I'd help her with Emily today." She thought for a moment. "Maybe you can ride with us."

Pam's face brightened. "Let me go ask," she said. And with a bounce and a twirl of her calico dress, she ran to find her mother.

The Barneses, along with Pam, rode through Portsmouth. They turned up Pleasant Street and drove through Market Square. Normally the city was quiet on Sunday afternoons, but that day there were horses and buggies everywhere.

"Why is it so busy today?" Sarah asked her father, looking out at the bustle of activity.

"Mr. Polk, one of the men running for President, is here campaigning for the election," said Mr. Barnes, steering the horses to the right. "Keep your eyes open, girls, and you may just see him."

"Mr. Barnes," said Pam excitedly. "We might see the next president."

"That's right," Mr. Barnes said with a laugh. "You certainly might."

Mr. Barnes drove the horses along Bow Street toward Liberty Park. Sarah and Pam looked carefully, but to their dismay they didn't see Mr. Polk anywhere. They did not know then that he would become the next President of the United States.

\* \* \* \* \*

"Thank you for lunch, Mother," Sarah said. Pam helped her pile the dishes back into the picnic basket. "We're going for a walk now."

"Fine," Mrs. Barnes answered. "Take Emily with you."

Sarah wiped potato salad off Emily's cheek. "Do you want to go for a walk?" she asked her.

Emily twirled around and around in a circle. "Yes, please! Yes, please!"

Sarah and Pam stepped onto the cool green grass. Emily started to run but came to a sudden stop. She almost crashed into Mrs. Cooper.

Mrs. Cooper was startled. "Ooh," she said, waving her fan briskly in front of her face. Emily ran and hid behind Sarah. Mrs. Cooper frowned and looked down her nose at Sarah's mother. "Hello, Mrs. Barnes," she said without smiling.

"Hello, Mrs. Cooper," Mrs. Barnes said with a smile, struggling to stand. She wiped a stray piece of hair from her forehead. "We are certainly having a warm summer," she said pleasantly.

Mrs. Cooper looked down at Mrs. Barnes's enormous stomach. "Yes, we are," she said waving her fan again. "Imagine, having another baby, when the end of the world is coming so soon!" she said. "Whatever shall you do?"

Sarah pulled Pam's elbow. "Let's keep walking," she whispered. She didn't want her mother to think that she was eavesdropping. She tried to walk away, but Emily clung to her skirt.

"As I'm sure you know, Mrs. Cooper," Mrs. Barnes answered coolly, "each child is a gift from God. His timing is not ours, and this child is a part of His great plan!"

"But of course, my dear," Mrs. Cooper said. She sounded as though she felt sorry for Mrs. Barnes.

"Good day, Mrs. Cooper," Mrs. Barnes said, turning away and sitting down on her blanket. Her face was flushed.

# Summertime Fun

"Humph," Mrs. Cooper said. The ribbons on her bonnet rocked back and forth as she waved her fan in front of her face. She stepped around Sarah and Pam, her head high in the air.

Sarah picked up Emily and carried her. "That was embarrassing," she whispered to Pam.

"Mrs. Cooper is a mean lady," Pam said. "Your mother was right."

Sarah smiled. What Pam had said was true. She was proud of her mother. Setting Emily back down in the green grass, she heard shouts and laughter being carried through the heavy summer air toward them. Next to the pond, a group of boys were running in a three-legged race.

"Let's go and see who's winning," Pam suggested, and skipped toward them.

Sarah took Emily by the hand, and together they ran after Pam. They pushed their way to the front of the small crowd that was gathered to cheer on the racers. Sarah sat down cross-legged on the grass, Emily on her knee. She watched as Peter and David tried mightily to get to the front of the race. Peter was almost carrying David along. It looked as though they might win until David tripped and landed on his nose.

Sarah and Pam giggled.

"Poor David," Pam said. "Peter is too strong for him."

Peter lifted David off the ground, and they ran on again and came in fifth. Sarah and Pam cheered for them.

"Sarah! Sarah!" Katie pushed her way through the group of people and sat down on her knees next to Sarah.

"What is it?" Sarah asked.

"Mother is tired. She wants you to go and get Father, and tell him that it is time to go home," Katie said, panting. "I'll sit with Emily."

"Why can't you go and find Father?" Sarah asked. She didn't want to leave. They were just starting another race.

# Summertime Fun

"Mother doesn't know where Father is, and she said that she doesn't want me to go 'romping aimlessly all over the park'."

Sarah frowned and pushed herself up to her knees. "Fine," she said. "Go back to the blanket as soon as this race is over."

Sarah marched across the park. She finally found her father in a quiet corner of the park under a big shady tree. He and Pastor MacMillan, Mr. Van Dyke, Mr. Cooper, and several other men stood talking with their Bibles open in their hands.

Sarah patiently waited until no one was speaking.

"Excuse me," she said in her most grown-up voice. "Father, Mother would like to leave now."

Mr. Barnes smiled down at her. "Right now?" he asked. "I'm in the middle of something important."

"I'll tell her, Father."

Mr. Barnes looked up at the other men. "I'll be there in a few minutes," he said to Sarah.

# A SECRET IN THE FAMILY

"Yes, Father," Sarah answered. *I hate being the oldest,* she thought. *I hate being everyone's messenger.* She sulked as she walked through the trees and across the park.

Katie and Emily sat on a corner of the blanket next to their mother. They sat very quietly. Sarah plopped down beside them. "I told Father," she reported.

"Thank you," said Mrs. Barnes weakly. Her face was no longer flushed, but pale. She rubbed her lower back slowly up and down.

Sarah pulled a blade of grass and blew it like a whistle.

"Please don't do that," Mrs. Barnes snapped.

Gloomily, Sarah dropped her whistle. She sat quietly with her legs folded up against her chest until her father arrived. It seemed as if he was taking forever.

"Pastor MacMillan has left me no choice, dear," Mr. Barnes said, placing his

Bible down on the blanket. "He says that we have been proven wrong because Jesus hasn't come back yet. He says that our theology is wrong. I really think that it's time we take our stand and leave the church. We've been talking about it for a while, and now is the time for action."

Sarah wasn't sure that she had heard right. *Father didn't really say that we have to leave our church, did he?* she asked herself. She was horrified. She didn't have time to think about it, though, because suddenly Mrs. Barnes let out a long cry.

"Edward," she said sharply. "Stop talking. This is not the time to be discussing this. I'm in labor!"

Mr. Barnes looked stunned. "But—but the baby isn't supposed to be here for almost three more weeks," he stammered.

Mrs. Barnes grabbed her side. "I guess it doesn't know that," she said. "Let's get home."

## CHAPTER 6

# A
# New Baby

In the early morning hours of July 26, 1844, a soft cry filled the Barneses' household. It was the cry of another healthy newborn.

Sarah and Katie sat wrapped in Sarah's quilt on the parlor couch. The brave little cry woke Sarah out of her half sleep.

"The baby," she said, shaking Katie.

Katie blinked her eyes and sat up. Together the sisters listened in awe and wonder to the newborn's cry. "The baby is finally here," Katie whispered. "I can't believe it."

"Me neither," said Sarah. She snuggled in close to her sister. A door gently opened and closed upstairs. Soft footsteps came down the hall. It was their father. He wiped his forehead and his hands with his handkerchief. The house was warm, even in the middle of the night.

Mr. Barnes looked at his two oldest girls. A twinkle danced in his eye. "It's a boy!" he cried.

Sarah felt very happy. She and Katie hugged, and then jumped up and hugged Mr. Barnes. A boy! Sarah couldn't wait to see her little brother.

"May we go and see him?" Sarah begged. "Oh, please, Father."

Mr. Barnes laughed. "Let your mother rest for a little while," he answered. "The doctor is still in with her." Mr. Barnes stretched. "The sun will be up soon," he said, looking out of the window. "Run up-

# A New Baby

stairs and sleep for a little while." Mr. Barnes scooted them up the stairs. "I'm going to try and get a little sleep myself," he said, and stretched out on the sofa.

Sarah climbed into her bed. The sheets felt cool and refreshing. She couldn't sleep. She held Henrietta and counted the stars in the sky outside her window. A voice whispered at the bottom of the stairs.

"You have a healthy little son, Mr. Barnes." It was Dr. O'Connor.

"Thank you, doctor," Mr. Barnes answered sleepily. "Have a safe trip home."

Sarah listened as the front door opened and then softly closed. The house was quiet once again.

Sarah tried desperately to fall asleep, but the harder she tried the more awake she was. Finally, she couldn't stand it any longer. She tiptoed past Katie's bed, through the door, and out into the hall. She stood outside her parents' bedroom door for a minute. Not hearing any noise, she carefully turned the doorknob and tiptoed into the room.

"Sarah, is that you?" Mrs. Barnes quietly asked.

Sarah was startled. "Sorry to wake you, Mother," she said. A candle burning on the bedside table lit a path to the bed.

"You didn't wake me," Mrs. Barnes said, rolling over to look at Sarah. "I've been lying here admiring our perfect little baby."

"I couldn't stand it any longer," Sarah whispered. "I have to see him."

Mrs. Barnes smiled and carefully pushed herself up into a sitting position. Sarah sat down at her feet. Ever so gently her mother lifted the tiny bundle from beside her and placed the sleeping baby in Sarah's arms.

Sarah looked down at her brother's perfect little face. His skin was purple and red and wrinkly. Still, Sarah thought that he was the most handsome creature in the whole world.

# A New Baby

"Oh, Samuel," she whispered. "You are the most wonderful brother I could ever have hoped for."

Mrs. Barnes softly giggled. "Samuel," she said. "I like that."

* * * * *

The following Sunday morning Sarah put on her best dress. She pulled at the sleeves and straightened the collar. She untied the rags she had used to curl her hair and gently smoothed the curls. Then she pulled the curls into a big ribbon at the back of her head.

Katie pushed open the bedroom door. "Sarah," she said, holding out her brush, "will you please do my hair for me? Mother is nursing the baby and says she can't."

"Come here," Sarah said. She sat down on the edge of the bed, and Katie sat on the floor in front of her. Sarah untied Katie's rags and ran her fingers through the blond curls. She pulled the curls up into a bow as she had done for her own.

"Thank you," Katie said, inspecting Sarah's work in the mirror.

Sarah and Katie hurried downstairs. Sarah pulled out her mother's best dishes and the special linen tablecloth. The new baby's dedication service would be held that day. Sarah felt happy, but she was also very sad. Her mother and father had decided to leave the Methodist church. Sarah still didn't really believe it. She couldn't imagine not going there each Sunday morning. But the Barnes family was not alone. The Van Dykes and two other families had also decided to leave. Pastor MacMillan and many of the church elders, including Mr. Cooper, felt that they were wrong and that the Second Advent wasn't coming soon. The Barneses, the Van Dykes, and others still clung to the hope that Jesus would return soon. They would not give up.

# A New Baby

Sarah dashed outside the house and down the wooden stairs that led to the cold room. She reached for the tray of squares she and Katie had prepared the night before. Carefully she carried them back up the stairs and closed the door behind her.

"Do you need some help?"

Sarah blinked in the sunshine. It was Pam. "Thanks," she answered, handing the tray to her. "Go and put these on the table. I'll get the next tray."

With Pam's help, Sarah and Katie had the house looking just right as people began to arrive.

Mr. Barnes slipped in through the kitchen door. "Sarah, please put these in a vase," he said, handing her a big bunch of flowers.

"Father, they're beautiful," Sarah exclaimed as she reached for them.

"Fresh from the meadow," Mr. Barnes said, beaming. "They'll make your mother smile."

# A SECRET IN THE FAMILY

Sarah found a vase and gingerly carried the flowers out to the dining table.

"Sarah," Pam said. "Look who is here."

Sarah nearly dropped the vase. She stumbled and awkwardly set it on the table. Pam was standing arm in arm with Alannah. Sarah couldn't believe her eyes. She didn't know what to say.

Alannah let go of Pam's arm and stepped toward Sarah. A stray red curl slid over her forehead. "My mamó made a blanket for your brother," she said, handing Sarah a soft package tied with a ribbon.

"Thank you," Sarah said.

"I'm sorry," Alannah said hesitantly. "I guess I started to believe all of the mean things Nickie was saying. I shouldn't have. She only cares about herself." Alannah looked over at Pam. "You two are my friends. My best friends."

Sarah's lips quivered. Tears of joy spilled onto her cheeks. "Oh, Alannah," she said, hugging her friend. "I forgive you."

# A New Baby

Alannah wiped a tear from her cheek.

Pam took each of them by the hand. She grinned, and her eyes sparkled. "Now, enough of this mushy stuff," she said.

They all giggled.

"What's so funny?" Katie asked. She licked some icing off her finger.

"Katie," Sarah scolded, "you aren't supposed to eat the squares yet. Those are for after the dedication."

Katie pouted and looked at the floor. One of her curls slipped out of her hair ribbon and onto her face.

"Katie," Alannah said, "who did your hair? Come with me. I'll fix it."

Katie smiled. "Sarah did it," she said, making a face at her sister.

"Well, that explains it," Alannah teased. She winked at Sarah and led Katie into the parlor.

Pam and Sarah sighed happily.

"Everyone," Mr. Barnes announced. "Please join us in the parlor. Our little son is happily asleep in his mother's arms. We would like to have the dedication before that changes!"

Laughter rippled through the house, and everyone gathered in the parlor. Mrs. Barnes sat in her husband's chair, holding the baby. Sarah sat on the floor in front of Grammy and Emily. She watched her mother's face. She looked happy. *I wonder if she looked that happy when I was born,* Sarah thought. She smiled to herself. She was sure that she had.

Mr. Barnes stood in front of the hearth. "Thank you all for coming to our home. We are here this morning because we are without a church to worship in. But even without a church we will worship God. We praise Him for His blessings."

Mr. Barnes helped Mrs. Barnes stand up. "We are gathered today to dedicate our son, Samuel Joseph Barnes, to God."

Mrs. Barnes winked at Sarah. Already, the name Samuel seemed to suit him perfectly.

# A New Baby

Mr. Barnes held out his arms and took baby Samuel from his mother. He smiled down at the sleeping face. "Please stand with me as we pray."

Sarah stood up and folded her hands and closed her eyes. She felt happy and peaceful. She felt as though her family was now exactly how it was supposed to be.

"Dear heavenly Father, thank You for this, our fourth child," Mr. Barnes prayed. "Thank You that he is a happy and healthy child. This morning we dedicate him to You. We pray that he may be a blessing to Your work. We pray that we may be found to be honorable parents. We thank You for his life." Mr. Barnes paused, and his voice shook a little. "Even so, Lord Jesus, come."

# Get the whole Adventist Girl Series!

These stories about a young pioneer girl named Sarah Barnes take children back in time to the days of William Miller between 1842 and 1844. Even as Sarah's family accepts the message of Jesus' soon return, Sarah must keep up with her daily chores and school-work. This four-book historical series will entertain and educate children about the Adventist heritage and hope. 0-8163-1907-3, US$24.99, Cdn$38.99.

### Book 1. A Song for Grandfather.
Eight-year-old Sarah Barnes can't wait to see Grammy and especially Grandfather! She knows he'll tell her wonderful stories of his life as a sea captain. But Grandpa surprises the whole family with some startling ideas he heard William Miller preach from the Bible. *Jesus will return very soon and the world will come to an end!* Will they accept the message? Paper, 96 pages. 0-8163-1873-5.

### Book 2. Miss Button and the Schoolboard.
Sarah and her best friend Pam love school—except for those annoying boys and that mean girl Nickie Cooper! Their beloved teacher, Miss Button, is the best teacher in the world. Even so, it's getting harder to be a Millerite and the teasing gets worse. Paper, 96 pages. 0-8163-1874-3.

### Book 3. A Secret in the Family.
Paper, 96 pages. 0-8163-1887-5.

### Book 4. Sarah's Disappointment.
Sarah hears Samuel Snow preach that Jesus will definitely re-turn on October 22, 1844. Good news! New hope! Still, it's a hard time for Sarah. Some of her friends are now her enemies. Paper, 96 pages. 0-8163-1888-3.

Order from your ABC by calling **1-800-765-6955**, or get online and shop our virtual store at **www.adventistbookcenter.com**.
- Read a chapter from your favorite book
- Order online
- Sign up for email notices on new products